JER Eberts
Eberts, Marjorie
Pancakes, crackers, and pizza : a
book about shapes /
$4.95 ocm10724207

W9-ALN-843
3 4028 10019 9463
HARRIS COUNTY PUBLIC LIBRARY

A ROOKIE READER

PANCAKES, CRACKERS, AND PIZZA

A BOOK ABOUT SHAPES

DISCARDS

By Marjorie Eberts and
Margaret Gisler

Illustrations by Stephen Hayes

Prepared under the direction of Robert Hillerich, Ph.D.

CHILDRENS PRESS™
CHICAGO

To our mothers

Library of Congress Cataloging in Publication Data

Eberts, Marjorie.
Pancakes, crackers, and pizza.

(A Rookie reader)
Summary: The things that Eddie loves to eat all come in different shapes. Includes a word list.
[1. Shape—Fiction. 2. Food—Fiction. 3. Vocabulary]
I. Gisler, Margaret. II. Hayes, Steven, ill.
III. Hillerich, Robert L., 1927- IV. Title.
V. Series.
PZ7.E194Pan 1984 [E] 84-7699
ISBN 0-516-42063-1

Copyright ©1984 by Regensteiner Publishing Enterprises, Inc.
All rights reserved. Published simultaneously in Canada.

Printed in China

45 46 47 48 R 21 20 19 18 62

Scholastic Inc., 557 Broadway, New York, NY 10012.

This is Eddy.

Eddy likes to eat, and eat, and eat.

CEREAL
DOUGHNUTS

Eddy eats round things.

Eddy eats pancakes,

oranges,

and eggs.

Eddy eats square things.

Eddy eats crackers,

CRACKERS
CRACKERS

meat,

and cheese.

Eddy eats triangles.

Eddy eats pizza,

salad,

and watermelon.

Eddy eats circles,

and squares,

and triangles.

Eddy eats all shapes.

Eddy eats, and eats, and eats.

Eddy looks

like what he eats.

WORD LIST

Harris County Public Library
Houston, Texas

		round
all	he	salad
and	is	shapes
cheese	like	square(s)
circles	likes	things
crackers	looks	this
eat	meat	to
eats	oranges	triangles
Eddy	pancakes	watermelon
eggs	pizza	what

About the Authors

Marjorie Eberts and **Margaret Gisler** have spent the last few years collaborating on books dealing with the language arts. Both have had experience as teachers and have masters degrees in reading from Butler University. This is their first Rookie Reader.

About the Artist

Stephen Hayes is a free-lance, humorous illustrator from Cincinnati, Ohio. He received his degree in Fine Arts from Miami University in Oxford, Ohio. Steve has illustrated humorous greeting cards and several books for children. This book is dedicated to his wife, Susan, and his daughter, Sarah.